FULL CIRCLE

CHUDNEY THOMAS

Cover Art, design and formatting by
Sweet 'N Spicy Designs:
http://sweetnspicydesigns.com

Editing by The Midnight Line Editor
http://www.midnightlineeditor.com

Full Circle/ Chudney Thomas. -- 1st ed.

ISBN-13: 978-1502507327
ISBN-10: 1502507323

Dedicated to my mother,

Noreen DeFreitas.

CHAPTER ONE

H e was home.

The whine of the automatic garage door set Ria Marlett's body trembling. Like the coward she was, she hid in the kitchen while everyone else moved to the front door of the sprawling Florida ranch that served as Pack Central and the Alpha's home.

The sound of kids squealing in delight brought Ria's head up in the middle of counting silverware. She imagined he was tossing his nieces and nephews in the air, a huge grin on his face.

She shouldn't be here. If she'd known he'd be home in time to attend February's Pack Circle, she would have made sure that she wasn't. Now, she was stuck, hiding in the hope of avoiding talking to him. Hell, to avoid him even scenting her. Which was a vain hope, since as Alpha of his pack, Drake Neilson had the most acute senses of them all.

Ria eased through the butler's pantry into the

adjoining dining room and proceeded to set the table. It wouldn't get done, if she didn't do it. They had all wandered off, distracted by their Alpha's arrival, and most likely would stay away until they decided it was time to eat. Like the kitchen, the dining room was huge. It had to be. The Pack was huge. There were, at any given time, anywhere from sixty to a hundred members. Protecting them was the reason Drake had been away.

As one of the few humans in the Pack, Ria occupied an uncertain status. As the only orphaned member, she was in some ways even lower. Worse, she was attracted to him, the Alpha, Drake Neilson. She cut that thought off. In a pack full of werewolves, emotions had to be hidden deep. Or, personal scent had to be disguised. In fact, if she'd known he was going to be here, she would have doused herself in perfume.

Heavy footfalls sounded down the hallway. Ria kept her eyes and hands busy with the task of setting up the buffet table.

"Ria." Drake's deep voice rolled across her skin, setting her nerves on fire. She could almost hear his smile.

As she worked, she moved. It was instinct, to keep the predator in the room with her at bay. As she moved, his jean-encased thighs came into view. Her gaze was drawn up his long, lean, T-shirt-covered torso.

Ria swallowed. She didn't understand why he insisted she of all people meet his gaze and hold it. Pack etiquette dictated one made brief eye contact and focused somewhere else. Staring could bring out the aggression in a dominant wolf. It was a challenge to hold a wolf's gaze, yet Drake insisted she do it.

Ria knew better than to antagonize him, so she complied. His strong jaw was covered in dark stubble. His full lips stretched into a smile that sent her pulse racing. Green eyes held her captive as she felt her lips stretch into a tight smile. Her hands shook as she put the last of the water goblets on the table. She looked away.

"Welcome back, Drake."

***

Drake felt his wolf's aggression rising, and he hadn't even been home for half an hour. *She* barely looked at him. She hadn't come to greet him. For months, Ria had been keeping him at a distance. He remembered a time when those pretty brown eyes met his without hesitation. When her full lips would curve into a warm smile of welcome. He longed to caress her warm golden skin once more. Now, here she stood on the opposite side of the table, her dark hair tumbling free around her shoulders, poised to flee. He couldn't help it if he growled rather than spoke. "Is it all ready?"

She barely nodded in answer as she methodically finished setting the table. He couldn't get a clear read on her emotions. Uncertainty made his aggression worse.

Drake sucked in a breath. He needed to calm down. With each breath, he gathered more information. Ria's fear was tinged with lust. The scent of an unattached female approaching the dining room interfered with Ria's interesting scent. He stifled his annoyance at being interrupted. Ria slipped away as soon as his attention wavered. He let her go. It was more than obvious she didn't feel comfortable around him. It might have to do with the fact that every time he got close, he wanted to take her down and mark her. Maybe that showed.

Through the course of the night, as he grew frustrated at her absence from the table, from the living room, from everywhere he was, Drake reminded himself she was human. As a human, she didn't have the same instincts he did.

He'd finally spotted his prey on the screened-in patio by the pool when a less than delicate hand connected with his shoulder. "Stop scaring her."

James, his second, stood by his side. Drake had scented his approach, but had chosen not to acknowledge it. He let his gaze shift from where Ria was busy helping feed one of the Pack's many children. He smiled at the sight. Piles of clothing dotted the floor as the older kids gleefully romped in wolf form, as they had been given permission to change after eating their suppers. The hapless babies were the only ones left.

"She doesn't know how you feel," James said. "Tracking her every move is bound to make her feel hunted."

"Why would that make her feel hunted? Did you tell her that I'd be here?"

"I didn't tell her. Hell, I didn't tell anyone you'd be back tonight." James gestured in her direction. "If she knew, she wouldn't have been here."

Drake growled and James complied by voicing his next statement in more submissive but firm tones. "Look. She's human. She's part of the Pack, but not. The others treat her as a submissive. They've treated her that way since she was a teenager. Do you think that she doesn't know that?"

Drake stood to the side and watched as, one after another, mothers handed Ria their infants' bottles and diaper bags, readying themselves for an evening of enjoyment with the Pack. Ria was soon barricaded by a half-circle of infants in portable car seats. Still, more than one of the Pack stopped to request more food, more drink—just more, period. If something was missing, they looked to her to fix it. Ria filled an essential role. He wasn't sure that she knew it.

He frowned as one more person handed over

another diaper bag. Perhaps she filled her role within the Pack too well.

He searched the room and located a few of the younger unattached females and barked out a short order.

***

"Here I'll take *that* from you."

Startled, Ria looked up from the baby she was trying to feed as she rocked another one across her lap.

One of the Pack's females was holding out her hands impatiently. "Give me the baby. Trina will feed the other kid."

Ria frowned up at the two females standing side by side. Reluctantly, she handed over the two babies to the females and stood up from her chair. Her stomach rumbled. "Thanks."

She was hungry, but she didn't want to give up the shield the kids provided. If Drake saw her heading for the dining room, alone, then he would most definitely follow. A quick look around the room showed he was in deep discussion with James. Feeling every inch the coward, Ria decided to head for the kitchen, instead. Within two steps, however, her foot connected with a small furry pup who immediately butted her and demanded to be picked up.

She understood her duty to sooth the tiny hurt she'd caused, so she cuddled the little furry body close.

"Better?"

The pup's little tongue flicked out to lick her cheek, and Ria couldn't help but giggle. Soon, the young one tired of being held and wriggled to get down. Ria gladly complied, not wanting to lose her chance to get something in her stomach.

The kitchen was empty of Pack members as well as most of the food, but wonder of wonders, there was enough ham left over to make a sandwich. Ria's stomach rumbled again as she hastily built her sandwich.

The sound of the double dishwashers running almost drowned out the sound of the festivities in the great room. Almost. She took a sip of her Coke, hoping the carbonation and sugar would give her the energy she needed for the long night to come. She wasn't a part of the Pack, not really. She stood on the periphery. The only place she held in the Pack was the one she'd made for herself.

"Why are you eating in the kitchen?"

Drake. His voice rolled across her nerves, simultaneously setting them aflame and irritating them. She'd learned long ago to hide her physical pull toward his masculinity. He was her Alpha, so he'd never look at her that way in return. Any irritation she felt was only a result of her frustration with the situation between them. Besides, no one, especially not a half-human, challenged the Alpha.

***

Drake watched as she literally made herself smaller, never making direct eye contact with him as she huddled over her sandwich. Her black curls partially hid her face from view as she ate. It made him want to snarl and snatch her up from the chair. He had no idea what he'd do after that, so he stayed where he was. Humans were frail. She couldn't take what he was capable of dishing out.

"It was just easier to grab a bite in here." She cleared her plate and began emptying the first dishwasher that had finished running.

Drake didn't know what hit him. One moment, he was standing in the doorway. The next, he'd set her back from the dishwasher and proceeded to unload the damned thing himself.

"I can do that," Ria said. "It's your first night back, and besides, you're the guest of honor."

He felt her timid attempt to move him out of the way. He stiffened at the delicate touch of her hands on his spine, lust shooting through him. Ria noticed and immediately removed her hands from his body.

"I'm sorry. I shouldn't have touched you." She was backing away now. Her fear wafted through the kitchen, overriding the scents of food and Pack.

A bold female named Sheena appeared in the doorway. "Jeez, what the hell did you do now, Ria? I can scent your fear way out here."

He saw the calculation in Sheena's gaze as she joined them by the dishwasher. Sheena ran her hand down his spine with a confidence that should have been appealing. "Here, Drake, let me do that."

Drake caught the fleeting scent of jealousy and pain from Ria, just before she melted into the other room, disappearing into the Pack.

***

Ria dug deeper into her cavernous purse. Her keys had to be in here somewhere. She thought of the chaos in the great room and dug deeper. Ria needed her keys if she was going to escape Drake.

As she scrabbled around the bottom of her bag, she listened to the familiar whistle of a man who was not only second to the Alpha but also his best friend. She should have known that trying to sneak out was a ridiculous idea. Ria turned around to find James blocking the door. Where Drake was dark James was light. Shaggy blond hair fell into hazel eyes. Eyes that missed nothing.

"Where do you think you're going?"

"I have to work tomorrow, remember?" He was her boss at CFP Construction and had been since she'd returned from college. He was also the one who'd helped her pick up the pieces after her mother had died in a car accident.

"What if I said you'd better serve the Pack by staying here tonight?"

He was joking; he had to be. She hoped.

James shook his head. "You should see the look on your face, Ria. You know running away from Drake isn't the best way to deal with him."

"I don't know what you're talking about." Ria resumed digging in her purse. "Have you seen my keys?"

"No, I haven't." He looked over her head and smiled. Ria's heartbeat picked up speed. She gripped her purse more tightly as heavy footsteps sounded in the hall. Warmth at her back told her just how close Drake was.

James shoved off of the door, a grin of amusement on his face. He had the audacity to wink at her as he brushed past her and sauntered down the hall.

"Aren't you going to tell me why you're leaving?" Drake asked. He wasn't growling at her anymore. His voice was as gentle as she supposed one could make gravel.

"I have tons to do tomorrow, and I'm tired. Feeding and cleaning up after forty Pack members and their assorted spouses and children isn't easy." She chanced a glance at his face and was surprised to see him frowning.

"Didn't you have any help?" He was beginning to sound angry.

"Well, yes. But most of the women are busy with their families and the unattached females really have no clue. Besides…" She bit her lip, not wanting to say more.

"Besides?"

She shrugged. "It's just what I do."

What she'd really meant to say was that no one paid attention to her when she issued an order or made a request for help with the kitchen or child-care. Well, almost no one. James would do whatever she asked, but she didn't like asking. Drake had always listened even when he didn't have time, but in the months since Ria had realized the attraction she felt for him wasn't a case of infatuation, she'd made a point of avoiding him.

"And that makes it okay that you are the one to

shoulder the responsibility?"

She dug back into her purse, uncomfortable with where the conversation was going. He was in alpha mode, solving a problem. The last thing she wanted to be to Drake was a problem. Her fingers connected with cool metal.

"With me here, they can focus on bonding. I don't—"

"We all take advantage of you," he continued, as if she hadn't spoken.

"This is my Pack, too, and this is where I fit."

Drake moved closer, his hands brushing hers as he closed the distance between them. Trembling, she stood her ground, her eyes focused on his mouth.

"Our Pack," he said.

His fingers brushed her cheeks as her hands clenched on the keys. Ria felt them bite into the palm of her right hand. Still, she leaned into his touch. His low growl made her half-closed eyes open. Ria took a step back, bringing her purse up between them as he followed. "I have to go."

He stopped when her purse connected with his chest. She held it between them like a shield. She needed to leave before she did something stupid like give in to the need to touch him.

"Goodnight, Drake," she whispered as she slipped by him, feeling his fingers graze her hip as she went.

***

Drake strode through the building, greeting Pack mates and workers alike on his way up to Ria's office. He stood at her open doorway, captivated by the scene before his eyes. Timid, shy Ria was arguing with a supplier. Her hair was pulled away from her face in a ponytail. Her feminine body was encased in a pair of jeans that hugged her like a well-worn glove. She perched on the edge of her wide desk with the phone to her ear, her booted foot swinging, her face turned away from him.

"I need those fixtures. Marco, you do realize that if our reputation is damaged that will also trickle down to you? I would hate to see our business relationship go sour because you promised something you couldn't deliver."

Unashamedly, Drake eavesdropped. Ria had claws and she was sharpening them appropriately on someone who thought she was a pushover. Pride bloomed in his chest and with it confirmation of what he'd always known followed. Ria was strong enough to rule his Pack by his side. Now he just had to convince her of it.

"I expect to see them on Monday, Marco, or I'll find a new supplier." She ended the call, gave a self-satisfied little hum, and jumped down from the desk. Her eyes met his in the polished glass that separated her from the rest of the construction office.

He watched as her eyes widened and her spine stiffened.

He walked in and shut the door behind him.

"Drake. What can I help you with?" She covered it well, but now that her scent wasn't covered by the Pack or the scents of a warm kitchen, he scented her instant arousal—with fear and caution thrown into the mix. Her pulse beat faster at the base of her throat as he moved closer.

His wolf was triumphant. At last, she recognized him. He scented her panic and swooped in, determined to nip it in the bud. His hand closed on her neck. The curls at her nape tickled his palm. Drake wrapped her ponytail around his fist as she tried to back away. A brief warning growl left his lips as they covered hers in a soul-searing kiss.

***

Ria couldn't think. She could only feel as his lips moved over hers. Her mouth opened under the unrelenting pressure, and she was rewarded with the addictive taste of Drake. As her head fell back against the wall, Drake's arms were the only things that prevented her from sliding down toward the floor. Her hands clenched and unclenched in his shirt as she attempted to pull him closer. His right hand gripped her hip and it didn't take much for Ria to wind one of her legs around his.

He moved on to her neck and left her gasping for air as she threaded greedy fingers through his hair to cup his skull. She couldn't let him go, didn't want to. She used the wall for leverage and ground against him, trying to relieve the pressure that was building at the juncture of her thighs.

He groaned and pulled her tighter to him. Lifted her up so that both of her legs were wrapped around his waist and the heat of him was resting against her core. She needed more. She wanted his hands on her. That was, until she turned her head to the side. It took her a few seconds to realize that she was staring straight into James' glowing yellow wolf's eyes.

Panic hit. The hands she'd used to hold Drake close frantically pushed him away. "Let me go." She shoved at Drake's chest; he wouldn't budge. In fact, he buried his face in her neck. "Drake, we're in the office." The guys downstairs had gotten an eyeful. Her legs were still wrapped around his waist and his hands were still on her ass. *This isn't happening. This is never happening again.*

She unlocked her legs. "Drake?"

He growled a little, lifted his head and released her. Her legs slid to the floor. There was just enough space to slide by him. From the corner of her eye, she could see the guys moving slowly back to work. James must have given them the rough edge of his tongue. She concentrated on that while she waited for her heart to slow, and she attempted to put her-self to rights.

"Look at me." Drake's voice was nothing more than a low pitched growl.

She couldn't do as he asked. She was well aware that her hair was now falling out of her ponytail. Her hands shook as she straightened her shirt.

"Look at me."

He was right behind her. She turned and looked up into his narrowed, heated gaze. "Please leave." Her voice sounded thin and reedy. Her heart was back to pounding.

Two things happened: Drake snarled at her and James entered the room. James didn't get in between her and Drake physically, but instead spoke a single word.

"Drake."

It was a warning, nothing more, but one that made Drake pull back and in the end, slam the door as he left.

She couldn't look at James. She ran a shaky hand over her face. "I...I'm headed home for the day." There was no way she would be able to work like this. Her entire body was shaking and she couldn't look her coworkers in the eye. No one else but James knew she was in love with Drake. Had been for ages. At least, no one else had known before that kiss. Now, she was afraid everyone knew.

***

Drake could have kicked himself. He'd messed up royally. He tried to regain control, here in the alley behind the office building, pacing like a caged animal, kicking at the wall because he couldn't kick himself.

Angry footsteps were his only warning. The door to the alley slammed open and chunks of concrete hit him in the back.

"What the hell were you thinking?" James was pissed. He had every right to be as the brother-figure for Ria. "She's scared shitless."

Drake tamped down on his instinctive snarl. This wasn't an attempt by James to take over the Pack; this was James acting as not only his friend but Ria's. With James, Drake didn't have to worry about challenges to his leadership. James was unwaveringly loyal.

"I messed up."

"Yeah. You did. What were you thinking?"

Drake turned to face his best friend and second. James' eyes were slowly fading from yellow back to brown. They narrowed on the hand Drake knew was shaking as he ran it through his hair.

"I came close to just taking her."

"I know that. Hell, the entire crew knows it. Even the humans."

Drake shook his head even as a growl broke free of his throat. "Drive me home."

He tossed his keys to his second and waited. James grunted and moved around to the driver's side of the truck.

He'd just reached for his seat belt when James spoke up.

"I know you're going after her. Just find your control before you go hunting her again."

CHAPTER TWO

Hours later, in the privacy of her duplex, Ria was still shaking.

She'd half expected Drake to be waiting on her doorstep when she'd driven home from work. Since he hadn't been there, he must have satisfied that primal lust somewhere else. The thought of him sleeping with another woman hurt. The pain didn't stop her from wanting him.

James hadn't checked up on her again, either. She was grateful that she wasn't forced to face the guys. She didn't want to imagine what they thought of her now. She'd always maintained a distance. When anyone hit on her, she'd played it off. Now, Drake had all but had her clothes off in the office.

Curled up on the couch watching some brainless show was going to be the highlight of Ria's night, and that was good. No, she didn't need an oversized Alpha on her doorstep or in her bed.

But she wanted it.

The phone rang, waking her out of her light doze. Belatedly, she realized it was her cell and not the house phone. She grimaced when she saw the name: Sheena. "Hello."

She would love to pretend that she didn't know what Sheena wanted, but it was a Wednesday night and it sounded like Sheena and her friends were in a bar.

"We need your help."

"Why?"

"We had way too much to drink and need a ride home."

Ria rolled her eyes. "Why call me? Take a taxi. The bouncer will call you one."

"Look, we know you. You'll get us home in one piece. Please, Ria."

Sheena never said please, ever. She must have been in a bad way. Thankfully, it was only ten. Ria had been called out much later. Sheena and the others had a bad habit of assuming Ria was available at all hours.

The truth was, it was Ria's fault. She was always available. She'd dated a little but had learned the hard way that dating a werewolf was hazardous to the heart. A mate would come along and take him right out of the picture before she knew what was happening. Human males, on the other hand, hadn't the slightest clue how to deal with the suddenly territorial males that would appear to protect her, males like James, who felt the need to check out anyone she dated who wasn't already in the Pack.

Ria sighed as she stared at the ceiling, willing her body to get up from her comfortable couch. She grumbled to herself as she pulled on her shoes and picked up her purse. It was frustrating to know that her only value to the Pack was that of chief cook and bottle washer. She'd better add obligatory designated driver to that list as well. Ria made her way to the door, hitting the switch for the porch light as she grabbed her keys from her favorite mother of pearl dish on her shelf in the entry way.

She stepped out into the cool night air and felt soothed. Fall, when it hit Orlando, was wonderful. Her street was lined with cars as usual and the scent of wood smoke from rarely-used chimneys was in the air. She shivered but decided against going back in for a jacket. A quick twist of the door handle showed the bottom lock of her home's door was engaged. With another twist, the key locked the top deadbolt. Ria stepped back into a hard wall of muscle. She shrieked. Firm hands grasped her arms. The contact made her gasp, her body immediately sensitized.

"Where the hell are you going?"

She tipped her head back, and had to look way up. Drake frowned down at her, his black hair falling into his ice-grey eyes.

"To pick up Sheena and some of the others from a bar."

He cursed, but it was so low she couldn't hear what he said, except for, "I'll drive."

"But…" She sucked in a breath when he grabbed her upper arm and all but lifted her into his SUV. "They're expecting me."

"Well they're getting *me*." He shoved the SUV into gear and reversed out of the driveway.

"Well, at least Sheena will be happy," she mumbled under her breath.

He cut her a look but remained silent until they

got on the road. "Do they always call you?"

She hesitated.

"Ria."

Why bother denying it? He'd know she was lying, anyway. "Not always, but yes, they call me often."

A tense silence filled the cab of the vehicle. She looked at him. His jaw was locked. He seemed to get grimmer with each minute that passed.

"Why are you angry? This is the way things work."

He shot her an inscrutable look but otherwise remained quiet.

Ria couldn't sit still. She tucked her hands between her legs to keep them still as she watched the headlights of the cars on the road go by. They pulled up outside of the strip mall that housed the bar. The parking lot was full, and a group of people stood on the sidewalk, laughing, talking, having a good time. One of them was hunched over on the curb, undoubtedly about to lose most of the liquor he'd consumed. Ria quickly focused on something else.

She was undoing her seatbelt when Drake

reached over and placed his hand over hers. "Wait here."

"But..."

"Stay here, Ria."

She watched him walk across the asphalt, weaving through the parked vehicles. Here, in the darkened cab of his SUV, Ria could drop the pretense of not being interested. In fact, she savored the way he moved swiftly and smoothly through the night, toward the neon glow of the Orange Grove's entrance.

Music blared as he opened the door and disappeared into the bar. She wondered if Sheena and her friends were still doing shots. The last time Ria had gone to pick them up, she'd had to coax one of them down from dancing on the bar. Maybe Drake would fare better.

Light and noise spilled out into night once again as the door opened, illuminating the palm trees that dotted the sidewalk. Drake strode out, hustling a disgruntled Sheena and crew across the parking lot. Fortunately, Sheena remained upright but the other two were just about falling down. Ria put her hand on the handle, ready to help, but Drake's glare stopped her. She watched as Drake unceremoniously poured the other two into the back seat.

"So, you called the big man on us," Sheena snapped. Alcohol had obviously impaired her judgment if she was talking like this in front of her Alpha.

Ria opened her mouth to reply, but Drake slammed into the SUV, cutting her off. "I was at her house when you called."

That shut up the females in the backseat. Ria kept her gaze steadily ahead as she asked, "Did you pay the tab?"

Drake cursed and jumped out, heading back into the bar.

"What did you do now, Ria?" Sheena slurred drunkenly from the backseat. Ria hazarded a glance in the rearview mirror. The other two were passed out cold. "How is it you always manage to piss off Drake?" She snorted and leaned forward between the seats. "I heard something interesting today. You were making out hot and heavy with some dude at the office." Sheena's laughter rocked the car. "I can't believe it. You."

"Sheena, how much did you have to drink?" Ria

was desperate to turn the conversation away from herself and Drake. It was bad enough that the guys had seen Drake kissing her. It would be worse if she had an affair with Drake and it ended. Especially if Sheena knew. Sheena would be sure to remind Ria constantly that she didn't have what it took to keep an Alpha like Drake satisfied.

Not that she was going to sleep with Drake. No, she didn't want to go through that heartache. Not when everyone would know about it.

The door opened. Drake slid in, in a darker mood than before. The tension filled the cab of the vehicle as it rolled over the hot tarmac, the dark broken by the occasional street lamp and the lights from the strip malls. Ria almost envied the two sleeping girls who couldn't feel the anger filling the vehicle. Drake didn't speak for miles, until he neared Sheena's apartment. "Since you're the one that's awake, relay this message to your friends in the morning. I want you in my office tomorrow. All three of you."

"Aw, Drake."

"I don't want you back in that bar again." His

voice got deeper with each word. Sheena, even in her state, had the sense to keep her mouth shut. Her Alpha's anger was clearly enough to start sobering her up.

Drake pulled in the parking lot of the Pack-owned apartment complex. This time, Ria ignored his look and hopped out of the SUV into the cold Florida weather. He snarled at her, but Ria held her ground. Sheena exited the backseat first, eyes down and head averted. Ria looked on in amazement. This was the most submissive she'd ever seen the female.

Ria closed the doors of the SUV as Drake and Sheena wrangled and carried each of the severely intoxicated females up the three flights of concrete steps. Ria made a note to call the superintendent. A few of the exterior lights were flickering.

Wind cut through the breezeways, causing Ria to shiver. Ria stepped forward to relieve Sheena of the keys to the apartment. The door swung open and Drake wasted no time depositing his burden on the couch. Sheena, on the other hand, headed straight to the bathroom and deposited her Pack mate in the tub.

"She throws up." Sheena said by way of explanation.

Drake grunted a response and led Ria out of the apartment, but not before shucking his jacket and dropping it onto her shoulders.

"Tomorrow." He pulled the door closed behind them and hustled them back to his SUV.

Ria waited until they'd pulled away from the girls' apartment before she spoke.

"They're adults."

"Yes, and they should behave like it. You pick them up every Wednesday and Friday night?"

Her face flamed. "I don't always..."

"You do. Why are you always available?"

"I'm not always available."

"The bartender knows who you are and has your phone number."

Ria defended herself. "That's best for the Pack. I'm usually home."

"Why aren't you out enjoying yourself like they are?"

"I'm not into going out."

"That's not true. I've seen you out before."

Dread filled her. Dancing in the dark, surrounded by people who didn't know her name, was her guilty pleasure. Not even James knew that every so often she slipped away from her lonely home and the demands of the Pack and lost herself on a dance floor.

She kept her gaze on the darkened landscape. The wheels of the vehicle turned off the asphalt and onto her strip of a driveway.

Ria gathered her courage, miserable as she was to know her privacy had only been an illusion. "How long have you been following me when I go out at night?"

***

Great, now Drake knew he looked like a stalker. "I saw you dancing at Vida."

Vida was one of the few dance clubs she'd frequented, and since one of the Pack mates owned it, they always called him when Ria crossed the threshold.

She was watching him warily from the other

side of the cab.

"You were at Vida? Why?"

He hesitated, then went for it. "I went to see you."

"Me?"

He caught her incredulous glance. "Yes, you."

She bit her lip and turned her head away. He cursed silently, her scent of fear and confusion filling his head. He needed to go slow, but his wolf was howling for her.

"Why would you be looking for me?" Her anger was building, the scent slowly rising to wipe out the fear.

"I thought I was pretty clear this afternoon."

"I'm not a plaything, Drake. Go find another girl."

His vision went red. "Who said you were a plaything?"

"Isn't it obvious? You wouldn't look at me if I weren't convenient."

Drake flexed his hands. He forced himself to ease up so he wouldn't break the steering wheel. She hopped out of the SUV. He turned off the vehicle and stalked after her. She'd already closed the door to her house.

"Ria." He could hear her breathing on the other side. "Open up."

He put his palm to the door. He could take the door of its hinges, but scaring her wasn't in his plan. If he'd had a plan. Right now, he was winging it. The sound of her breathing propelled him into action. She was standing with just a few inches of door between them. "Ria. Open up. I watch you when you dance because you don't hide from me then. The only problem I have is that every other man in that club gets to see you, too."

He rested his forehead against her door and waited, surrounded by her scent and her things. A wind chime made a delicate sound every time a slight breeze blew past her porch. Just when he thought she would turn him away, he heard the tumblers of the lock disengage. He lifted his head and moved forward as she opened the door.

"What do you want from me?" She stood with her back to the wall, hand still on the door knob. Drake reached out and closed the door.

He didn't bother with a verbal reply. He swooped in, caging her body and claiming her mouth. She tensed, then melted against him. He groaned in triumph as heat coursed through his body. He wanted to lift her and wrap her legs around him. He did just that.

Her head fell back, and he feasted on her neck, enjoying the feel of her erratic pulse and the scent of her rising arousal. The knowledge of just how much she wanted him made it difficult for him to gain control of his wolf. His wolf wanted to claim her. Here, now, and to hell with the consequences.

The need to taste her rode him hard. He inhaled, and the scent of her drove him wild.

"Which way to your room?"

Her eyes were unfocused as he dove in for another kiss.

"Your bedroom?" he asked.

"The living room." She panted against his mouth.

The living room it was. His inner wolf didn't care.

***

Drake growled against her mouth. Ria's body felt as if it were a flame. When Drake made that sound, she melted for him. Something about that rumble that began in his chest caressed every nerve in her body, making her want more. He pushed her shirt up and began to nip at her belly. Consciousness began to surface as the cool air hit her stomach. Drake was working on her pants. *Oh no.* She pushed at his shoulders and somehow managed to be amused and exasperated when he wouldn't budge.

"No."

He looked up, his eyes glowing with the kind of heat she'd hoped for. Had hoped for, for years. Now, she was turning it down. Once she'd had him, he'd grow tired of her and move on to his next female, and then the next, until one day, he found his mate. Pain rolled through her at the thought.

He inhaled, frowned and sat up. "What did you just say?"

"No."

He moved away from the couch. "Are you telling me you don't want me?"

She looked away and hated the weakness that made her voice tremble. "No."

"That seems to be your favorite word tonight. If you want me, then why are we stopping?"

Ria let herself get angry. It was better to be angry than to give in to the need she felt for him. "Oh please. Don't try and tell me that I'm irresistible to you."

"You are." He was beginning to look frustrated now. "You've always been."

That hurt even more. "Give it up, Drake. Why me? You could have found anyone else to bed. Hell, you were at Pack Circle this past week. I'm sure that there were a bunch of unattached females who were interested."

"They are not you." He enunciated each word carefully, although he was growling now.

She took a good look at him. The wolf was out.

"Next, you'll be telling me I'm your mate." Ria pulled her shirt down from around her neck. "This is low, even for you, Drake. What? Did you forget that

I know all about mating?"

"What if that's what you are?"

"I'm not. Werewolves tend to mate with other wolves."

"What about your parents? Your father was a wolf."

"An anomaly. I'm one of the few humans in the Pack."

"Half-human and an integral member of our Pack."

"So I'm a freak. I'm half-werewolf with none of the benefits." She finished smoothing down her shirt. She rose.

"Ria, they trust you to take care of the pups. Our young are the most important members of the Pack, and no one in the Pack would hand them over to just anybody."

"No, I'm just a convenient babysitter, and I understand that it's my fault."

Ria skirted the edge of the sofa. If she could just get him to follow her, she'd lead him right out her front door. His large, warm hand closed over her shoulder.

"Look at me."

She did, making sure to meet his gaze, while moving backwards, drawing him closer to her goal.

"You are not a freak. Just because you're half human and half wolf, it doesn't mean that you're worth any less."

"Tell that to the Pack."

"It also doesn't mean," he continued, as if she hadn't spoken, "that you can't be my mate."

She'd succeeded in maneuvering him to the door. It was the hardest thing she'd ever had to do, but she wouldn't miss something she'd never had in the first place. She drew in a breath and ran her hand down the wooden door to the knob.

"Ria."

She pressed the thumb lock, and pulled the door open.

"Please leave."

***

Please leave. The words echoed in his head. He hadn't left her driveway just yet. He couldn't make himself. He'd wanted to pick her up and show her exactly how he felt. Problem was, he would have damaged his chances with her.

He'd backed away once, letting her go to college when he'd wanted her for his own. He'd given her a chance at a normal, everyday life. Ria may not have known it, but when she had chosen to return to the Pack, he'd known the time to claim her had come.

The scent of her fear and frustration when she'd asked him to leave had caused him to freeze. He was hurting her and he wasn't sure how he was doing it. The blank look in her eyes had made him want to tear something apart. That wouldn't solve his problem, either.

Ria was his mate. His wolf kept calling for her, and it was all he could do to keep the beast within him chained. He had to, until he convinced her that what he felt was real. That what he felt was more than lust. Otherwise, he would never have her. His chest ached with the need to let the sorrow out.

Sitting here in her driveway wouldn't win him points either, but he couldn't make himself leave. Knowing that she routinely rescued members of the

Pack from themselves both irritated him and made him proud. She cared for their Pack, although they'd taken advantage of her.

He gripped the steering wheel carefully and backed out of the driveway after one last look at her house. One thing was for sure: he wasn't giving up. She was his mate. He felt that ache in his chest whenever he looked at her as if the mate bond was already anchored in him. Now he just had to have it anchor in her. Eventually, he was going to convince her of it.

CHAPTER THREE

Ria wasn't sure she should be at work. James knew what was happening between her and Drake. Then, there was the construction crew. Until now, she'd never given any of them the slightest hint she was interested in dating. With James watching over her, she'd avoided any unwanted advances. Now the entire office knew that not only was she available but she was interested in the Alpha and he in her. It made for a potentially embarrassing situation, especially when it ended.

Damn it. He'd ruined everything. Her life up until now had been simple, just the way she'd liked it. Now she had to contend with a horny Alpha who seemed convinced there was a possibility that she was his mate. She opened the door to her office, which swung open smoothly and silently, just the way she liked it. Head down, she headed toward her desk.

She didn't want to look through the glass to see

43

her coworkers. The guys were watching her every move. Her face flamed. Worse than that, she knew exactly what they were thinking.

"Hey! You okay?"

She tensed and paused before she turned around. James leaned against the doorjamb, looking as if at least he'd had a good night's rest.

"I'm fine," she said.

"You don't look fine." He pushed off and walked forward.

She backed up a step.

James didn't stop until he was right in front of her, his head cocked to the side. "I'm surprised you're in today." It wasn't a statement. It was a veiled question. James excelled at that. He leaned in and sniffed.

She stuck her chin out. Just because she'd had a crush on Drake since high school didn't mean she would or had to sleep with him. "Why wouldn't I be here?"

He crossed his arms over his chest. "Funny, I didn't think he'd let you walk away."

Ria turned and walked toward her desk. James' stare felt like an itch between her shoulder blades.

She knew he wouldn't leave her alone until he got an answer that satisfied him. James was like that, a dog with a bone.

"Who says I let her walk anywhere?"

Ria spun away from the desk. Drake stood in the doorway, dressed in a pair of faded jeans and a button-down shirt. He took her breath away. She hated the way her body immediately reacted to him. In a rush of panic and retaliation she asked, "Who says that you have the right to let me do anything?"

James chuckled and moved to her side. She shot him a look and he grinned at her. "I never get between a wolf and his mate."

She crossed her arms and spat out from between gritted teeth. "Will you two stop? I'm not his mate. He's just horny."

James laughed and headed to the door. "You just keep thinking that. Good luck." He clapped a hand on Drake's shoulder as he left the room.

Drake advanced and maintained eye contact with her as he did so. In their world, it was a challenge. If he thought she was going to cower and lower her eyes, he could think again. Instead, she raised her chin.

"I thought you understood that I didn't want to see you again," she said.

"I thought you understood that you're my mate."

She sought refuge behind the desk—not that it offered much in the way of protection from Drake, but at least it was a physical barrier of sorts. It gave her enough of a sense of security that she continued to challenge him. "You and I know that when you mate, you have to mate someone strong. Someone capable of ruling the Pack."

"And you think you're not strong enough."

She sat in her chair. "I'm a low-ranking member of the Pack. No one takes me seriously except to make sure meals are out on the table and babies are taken care of."

"What about the fact that you manage to keep this crew—" He waved his hand toward the window. "—this crew, in line. That's no mean feat."

She laughed. "It's easy when James is always around to watch my back. There are a lot of guys who don't want a female managing them. Plus, I don't go out in the field."

"They respect you. You don't bullshit them."

"No, but what's the use of doing that? They work hard, they get paid, end of story." She leaned back, because at that moment he chose to sit on the edge of her desk, his hand closing over the snow globe she kept there. The snow globe he'd given her years ago. It was the first gift he'd given her at a Pack Circle, the first circle she'd attended after her after her father had died.

"It's more than that. You take care of the crew, of their families." He turned the snow globe between his palms. "You do the same thing with the Pack."

She frowned up at him. "I just do what I can."

He laughed at her, and immediately, she felt defensive. It wasn't as if she set out to take care of everybody. It just happened that way.

When she said as much, he laughed again. "You have no idea, do you? That's special. It takes a lot of grit to take care of a pack of werewolves."

"That doesn't make me Alpha material."

"Do you think being Alpha means you have to stare down every wolf in the vicinity? It means being smart enough to protect and nurture your pack." He slid off of his perch and held out his hand.

She stared at it, uncertain of what he was asking.

"Come on, I cleared your day off with James."

"I didn't ask for the day off."

"I know, but seeing as you view yourself as human, I decided that I have to court you before I can claim you as my mate."

She stood, but still didn't take his hand. "I never said I wanted to be courted."

He leaned in. Before she knew it, his hands were around her waist. She stared into his eyes, afraid to hope that he might be telling the truth. Afraid that she would wake up and it would be a dream.

He leaned in and did the unexpected. He rubbed his nose against hers. "You think I'm playing with you. Will you at least give me a chance to show you I'm not?"

She heard herself whisper, "All right."

***

She'd kept the snow globe.

Drake knew he had a chance. He'd have to hold

back, although he wanted to touch her, wanted to run his hand over her silky smooth skin and through that curly black hair. He sucked in a deep breath, tinged with her familiar scent.

She was still wary of him. He'd have to romance her, which made things difficult. He would have to rein in his wolf, because he wanted this woman. With two werewolves, no one worried about romance. It was usually a whirlwind event. They caught each other's scent and everything took care of itself.

"What's making you frown like that?" She was looking up at him. He brushed back of his hand over hers and felt the shiver that ran through her.

"I was thinking that this mating business is more complicated than I thought." She looked as if she wanted to ask him something, but he caught that scent of fear again before she withdrew.

He turned his hand and captured hers in his. "I'm having a get-together in a few weeks. I was hoping you'd help me plan it." He watched her from the corner of his eye.

"Is that what this is about?"

"No. I'm hoping that you'll decide to be mine by then. So we can make a formal announcement." He smiled as she took a step back. "You still don't think I'm serious do you? I am."

"I thought you just claimed your mate." She tugged at his hand. He let her slide away.

"What, and have you pissed off at me? No thanks. I'd like to have my mate happy." She still had her purse on her shoulder. "Spend the day with me?"

***

So, Drake thinks I'm not a Beta.

Her mouth twisted in disbelief. Everyone sure treated her like one. If she wasn't submissive, what exactly was she? The question tortured her on the ride, so much so, that it surprised her when he pulled up in front of his home.

She wasn't sure what she was expecting, but it wasn't ending up at his house, Pack Central. Several cars sat out front and she recognized them all. Only Drake lived here, but for the Pack, it was a gathering place, which meant that it was never completely empty.

Drake slid out of his seat. Ria tracked his movement around the car via the side mirror. With a heavy sigh, she released the latch for her seatbelt and reached for the door, only to find empty air. He reached in and lifted her bodily out of the seat. Her body slid down his and was on fire by the time her feet touched the driveway. They were still close. Then he was stealing a kiss that was quick, hard, demanding, and conquering, all in one.

He raised his head and his eyes glowed. Ria's breath caught as a shiver racked her body.

"Come on. I wanted to kick back and relax with you. Get to know you."

She raised an eyebrow. "Is that code for watching a movie and jumping my bones?"

He grinned at her from over his shoulder. "Only if you let me." Then with her hand in his, he towed her toward the house.

The last thing she wanted to do was head into a house full of werewolves when she was trying to sort out her own feelings on the whole situation. She didn't know if she wanted to be courted. She might just want to be taken.

The moment Drake set foot in the house, he was approached by one of his sentries. Ria stepped back, only to have him squeeze her hand and pull her forward. He leaned down and whispered in her ear. "Wait here for me. I need to take care of sentry rotation."

She nodded and he took off for his office.

Ria looked around the living room and the Pack members who had congregated there. She wasn't sure if this was normal or not. Usually she was at work. After hours, she was busy with her own home or with whichever Pack member called her phone.

"Look who the Alpha dragged in."

Sheena. The last person Ria wanted to see or talk to, especially after last night. Not only did Sheena have her sights set on Drake, but she had also been busted by the Alpha, all because of Ria. Of course standing right behind her was Trina, a transfer from another pack. She, too, wanted Drake, which made it odd they'd decided they were fast friends.

Pack protocol dictated that Ria at least

acknowledge them. "Good morning."

Sheena and Trina were watching her eagerly. They probably thought she smelled like fresh meat. "What are you and Drake up to?"

"That's our business."

"Oh no! It's Pack business," Trina piped up. She moved forward. Ria tensed but held her ground. Judging by the malicious look on her face, Trina felt as if she'd gained the upper hand.

Ria defended herself the best she could. "Then you might have a right to know, if you were a member of this Pack."

Trina halted. "I'm a member of this Pack."

"Only if you find a mate or apply for formal membership. Your Alpha has to approve it. Right now, you're on the hunt for a mate. Since you haven't found one so far, you'll have to apply for another transfer and look elsewhere."

Trina didn't like that, because she let out a little feral growl.

Sheena put a restraining hand on her shoulder. Ria felt no victory, only relief, when Trina backed down. Drake might have insisted everyone in the

Pack learn how to fight in their human forms, but it didn't mean that Ria was capable of throwing more than a few blocks and trying to step out of the way.

"Just because you've suddenly hooked up with Drake doesn't mean you aren't a submissive," Sheena said. "Enjoy it while you can. I hear a few other females have requested transfers to this Pack since Circle."

Hope Ria hadn't known existed shriveled deep inside. Still, she wasn't going to let Sheena see that. "Well, I guess that means you'll be out of the running then."

Sheena jumped toward her. Ria darted to the side, but Sheena still managed to clip her, driving her hip into the edge of the couch.

"Shit, Sheena. You have a death wish?" One of the younger males entered the room from the billiards room, pool cue still in hand. Ria liked Paolo. A low ranking sentry just out of college, Paolo exhibited dominant tendencies. Most of the Pack, like the two females in the room, had a habit of mistaking his laid-back approach with weakness.

"Mind your own business, pup." Sheena barked.

"Follow your own advice, Sheena." He thumbed the tip of the pool cue as his eyes locked on Sheena's. He walked forward to stand in front of Ria, like a self-appointed guard.

"Sheena." Every one of them turned to the sound of Drake's voice. From the sound of it, he knew just what was going on. "Attacking a subordinate Pack member, the morning after I had to pull you out of a bar?" Drake turned to speak to the male who'd entered the room with him. "Damien, these are the two I was talking about."

"Sheena and Trina." Damien stepped forward. "Follow me."

Sheena's eyes grew wide, but she followed Damien out of the room without so much as a glance in Ria's direction. Trina sneered as she brushed past Ria. Paolo took up the rear.

Ria tucked her hand through Drake's arm. Trying and successfully getting him to turn in the opposite direction, she drew him away, but not before she heard Paolo say to Sheena, "And yet again she saves *your* ass."

***

Ria's soft, warm body was pressed up against Drake's side. He hid his smile as she hugged his arm close, her attempt to keep him from going back and dealing with Sheena. They both knew she wouldn't stand in the way of him disciplining a Pack member. He'd already established a reputation for being a fair leader, and any punishment he meted out would be equal to the infraction. He looked down at her as they walked side by side down the hallway. He drew in a breath and his wolf rolled in her sent, enjoying her growing reaction to being close to him.

His mate was in his home voluntarily. She was snuggled up to his side, and he was taking her to his den. He hoped it would be hers, too, one day soon.

The large, cherry double doors loomed before them. Ria stilled. He didn't pause as he pushed the doors open and welcomed her into his sanctuary. Other than Ria, no other female had ever been in this place. Ria had been here before, but only because James had been up to his usual games of trying to get her into the same room as Drake. James might be protective of Ria, but he'd known almost as long as Drake had that Ria was Drake's, and he'd made it his business to bring them together.

She stepped into the room and immediately executed a sharp turn to the right after spotting his king-sized bed through the open double doors. He smiled even as his body and wolf demanded that he take advantage of the bed. He closed the doors to the suite behind them, forcing himself to appear relaxed as his space filled with her scent.

She was nervous, turned on and wary. Her scent and body posture told him if he did the wrong thing, she would run. He did the least threatening thing he could think of. He sat on the recliner and let her take in the changes he'd made. The last time she'd been in his suite, the front room had been empty except of boxes. The bedroom had only held his bed and nothing else. Now, it was filled with cherry wood and leather. He hoped she liked it, especially since he'd decorated it with her in mind. She walked along the edge of the room, drawn as he'd known she'd be to the bookshelves. Her fingers trailed over his collection of books the way he hoped they would trail over his bare skin. Her head bent as she examined souvenirs of trips past. She didn't know that he kept the few gifts she'd given him close to his bed, and she probably wouldn't learn that today, either. He knew that he wouldn't get her in the bedroom to see the safe place he kept them.

She glanced up and stepped back from the fireplace. Her hair fell to the side as her head tilted in an effort to take in the sheer size of the television screen he had mounted above it.

"Is it big enough for you?" she asked.

He laughed. "I think so." His TV had been one of his first purchases. The second had been the recliner loveseat he was now splayed upon while she slowly circled the room.

Her fingers trembled as she dropped her purse on the old steamer trunk he used as a coffee table, but she bravely faced him. "I really like what you did with it. You know, adding furniture."

He fought the urge to jump out of the chair and wrap her in his arms. The imp he remembered was still there in the mischievous flash of a smile. Now he just had to make sure that she let her guard down more often. He stayed put and felt triumph when she slid into the recliner. He waited until the last moment to hit the button that made the legs rise.

She let out a yelp and shot him an accusing glare.

"I like my comfort."

She made a show of snuggling into the seat. "So I see. Leather?" She arched a look in his direction.

Drake tossed her a soft blanket he'd picked out. It was a lush brown color that reminded him of her eyes. It was tied with gold ribbon, a bow on top like a gift. He wanted her wrapped in that blanket and nothing else.

"I'm not cold." She said, even as she pulled on the end of the ribbon to release the blanket.

He reached out and took it from her. "No, but aren't you the girl who always had to have a blanket when we watched a movie?"

Ria stilled beneath his gaze, and his wolf took notice of the way she wouldn't meet his eyes. Her fingers trembled as she smoothed them over the soft surface of the blanket. Every time he revealed that he'd paid attention to her, she withdrew.

As he waited for his Ria to come out of hiding,

he turned away from her and started a movie he'd learned from James that she wanted to see. By the time she settled down enough to realize what he'd put on, she'd snuggled as far into the corner as she could get. His wolf had to be content with the heat that rolled off of her body as she slowly relaxed into the chair.

Eventually, she laid her head against the headrest and laughed at the actors. Drake felt the mating bond lock into place as she turned her head to laugh with him. Curls framed her face, softened by her full-on smile. He had to hold back his wolf as he tried to lunge forward to take what was his.

He smiled back at Ria and looked away, afraid she'd see the need that had him clenching the long-neck bottle in desperation. He was thankful that he'd already drained it dry when he heard the glass crack and felt the give of the bottle. He immediately rested the cracked bottle on the floor and feigned absorption in the movie, while he listened to her breath as it became slow and even.

CHAPTER FOUR

Drake watched Ria sleep as the early morning light seeped through the window blinds. She was snuggled into the corner of the sofa. It was obvious she hadn't had much sleep the night before. He'd seen the evidence of dark circles under her eyes. Drake had intended to take her out, but he'd changed plans when he'd seen how tired she looked. Wouldn't she love to know that? When he'd decided on a movie at the last minute, he hadn't banked on this many people being at the house.

Ria shifted and moved closer to his warmth. Drake gave in to the need to feel her in his arms. He brought his half of the recliner into a sitting position, reached over and lifted her into his arms. His wolf, restless all night with her so close by but not able to touch, settled down as she snuggled in. He hit the button again on his chair and laid back against the leather with his mate stretched out on top of him. Her head on his shoulder. Her nose tucked against his neck. Her small hand resting against his chest. The scent of her tugged at him and surrounded him. Inhaling, he rubbed his cheek against the top of her head and closed his eyes.

An insistent beeping brought his eyes open. Ria was still snuggled up to him, one hand on his chest, a leg thrown over his. He liked it, though he would have preferred to be naked in his bed. The beeping was coming from his phone, which he could locate by sound. He was grateful Ria kept sleeping. She probably couldn't hear the faint beep, because her hearing wasn't on the same level as his. Reluctantly, he disengaged himself from her. Without thinking, he lifted her, blanket and all, and deposited her on the bed.

Sure that she was comfortable and undisturbed, he closed the door to the bedroom behind him and checked his phone. "James?"

"Sorry to interrupt your date, but we've got a problem."

"What kind of a problem?" He began putting the loveseat back in order.

"More than one lone wolf was sighted within

our territory, and one of our younger males was involved a fight with at least one of them."

"Who? Is he okay?" Drake paused the DVD, in case Ria wanted to finish the movie. It didn't look like he'd have the time to today, after all.

"Yeah, Tim's okay, just young and stupid. Doc is looking at him right now."

"Where are you?"

"Over at Doc's warehouse. You coming?"

Drake heard the commotion in the background and silently cursed under his breath. "Yeah, I'll be there." He ran a hand through his hair and looked for a pad to leave a note.

***

James met him at the warehouse door with an apologetic smile. "Sorry to interrupt, but this needs an Alpha's touch."

Drake clapped him on the back as they moved together down the hallway. There were warehouses like this all over the city. When wolves hid in plain sight, it was necessary. "Not a problem. Ria's asleep, anyway." They were moving toward the main holding area when he felt the weight of James' gaze on his face. "She was tired, and scared."

"Scared?" A note of warning crept into James' voice. "Scared how, Drake?"

"She doesn't believe me when I say that she's my mate." A howl from inside the warehouse filled the corridor, breaking up any chance for discussion. "Doc's got Tim?"

"Yeah."

"So who is in the cage?"

The sound of something hitting the side of the cage, hard, echoed down the hallway. He and James took off at a dead run.

Drake skidded to a halt with James right beside him. The sentries guarding the cage had backed up, eyes wary as a wolf threw itself against the bars. Its body heaved each time it pulled back for another assault on its jail. The sentries kept their hands on their weapons, ready to hit it with tranquillizers or silver should the need arise, but the wolf was still in the cage where it was supposed to be. Drake was relieved but worried. If the lone wolf kept this up, he'd kill himself.

Drake took a quick look around. The other cages in Doc's warehouse were empty, used only when wolves who were a danger needed a secure place to heal. Doc's warehouse functioned as a half-way house at times. No one else was in danger from the werewolf that stood in front of him.

"Has he been like this since you picked him up?" Drake gestured toward the angry wolf in the cage. Teeth bared, it had backed away from the silvered bars to stare at him. Its mouth opened on a silent growl.

James nodded, not taking his eyes off the were-wolf. "Yes. You think he might be stuck?" He sounded doubtful.

Drake drew in a slow breath, sifting through the scents in the air. He detected something, though none of the usual array of drugs that messed up a werewolf's ability to shift.

"Stay back." It wasn't necessary, but he gave the command just in case one of his people became tem-porarily stupid. He attempted to make and hold eye contact with the captive. Most people thought in order to be Alpha, one had to be brutal. They forgot brains were a necessary part of the equation. It wasn't just a matter of being strong, it was a matter of being strong, smart, and able to meld the two together.

"Shift," he said, once the wolf focused on him. This wolf was scared. He was in unfamiliar territory, and he'd attacked one of the reigning Pack's juveniles.

Slumped against the cage, he gave a pitiful whine.

"Shift." Drake put more force behind the order.

Submissive wolves couldn't deny an Alpha. Lone wolves tended to be dominant, but how dominant depended on the strength of the Alpha of the area they hailed from. This one smelled of desert. Drake doubted he'd need to take this all the way to a fight.

"Shift."

The sound of bones shifting, the sight of skin and fur moving, followed Drake's command. Tired and frightened, the man looked up from where he crouched on the floor of the cage. He looked dazed, not at all alert.

"Who are you?" Drake asked, making no move to open the door.

The nude man didn't answer. Instead, he rested his head against the cement floor of the cage. His body slowly followed.

"He's passed out. Get some bedding in there. Let him sleep it off." Drake turned away from the cage and gestured for James to follow him. "I'm going to talk to Tim. Listen, the new wolf is not going to know where he is when he wakes up."

James shot him a puzzled look. "Drugs?"

"It has to be something new."

"Do we need Doc?"

"I'll send him here after I'm done with him."

***

"I swear, Drake. I wasn't looking for a fight. All I said to the guy was I'd never seen him before."

Drake waited. If one stayed silent, people tended to fill the void.

Tim was one of those people. "The next thing I knew, he was on me. Boy, am I glad that you taught us how to fight in both forms."

Drake gestured to Tim's arm. "When did he do that?"

"He just shifted in mid-fight, man, and latched on."

"When he first attacked, he didn't say anything?"

"No, he was just standing there one minute, and the next, his fists were flying, and then..." Tim swiped his good hand over his face, dislodging some of the dried blood. "Then he was in wolf form hanging from my arm." He held out his arm.

"You need to shift in order to heal, but not here." The sutures that doc had put in would hold if Tim changed, although they would bleed. Drake pushed himself to his feet. "Wait for me. You can change at the house."

The boy heaved a sigh of relief.

As they pulled into the ranch's drive, the smell of home-cooked food hit Drake's nose. Tim's stomach was growling, or that could be his.

"I hope this means that Ria's over," Tim said,

showing his first sign of enthusiasm toward anything. "No one else's food smells this good."

Drake detected infatuation there. He growled, startling both Tim and himself by the unexpectedly quick response.

"I know she's yours. I'd never poach." Tim slid out of the SUV, white from the loss of blood and the control it took to harness his wolf. "You just have to use your nose. Besides, she's too old for me."

Drake laughed. Tim was right, all he had to do was use his nose. His stomach rumbled again, reminding him that he sat in a truck while others enjoyed his mate's food and company.

He found Ria standing in front of his oven with her back to him. A wave of rightness and possessiveness washed over him as he took in the sight of her cooking in his kitchen. It was something she'd done countless times, yet every time he was amazed that he could feel this way about something so simple.

His mate doing what she always did so well, taking care of his Pack. Something others took for granted came instinctively to her. She turned around and he took in her flushed cheeks, her soft curls pulled up into a ponytail. The ponytail made him want to walk over and loosen it to let her curls cascade over his hands. It had been too long since he'd last touched her. He let his lips curve into a smile and was rewarded by a shy smile in response.

"Hi."

He stood still as her eyes searched his face and her scent turned to confusion, need and a trace of fear. It was always there, ever present after the death of her parents. Drake had been hoping to slowly erode it over time. It hadn't worked out like he thought it would.

Her eyes widened, and Drake new he had to rein himself in, especially since he was in a house full of werewolves with big ears. He made his way over to the oven, grabbing a pair of mitts on the way. He opened the oven door and his eyes confirmed what his nose had told him when he walked in.

"Mac and cheese."

"Yes and *fried chicken.*"

They shared a smile as a collective groan went up around the house. And for a minute, her fear disappeared. Drake held his breath, only to watch her fear return full bore. She lowered her eyes and slipped into a full panic.

***

This was nice. Too Nice.

Ria stared at her feet, willing her heart to understand that this was only the first date. In fact, it wasn't really a date to begin with.

She'd woken up to find herself alone but covered by his blanket. The same one he'd presented to her, tied with a bow. She'd almost panicked when she'd realized he was gone, and then she'd spotted his note and panicked, anyway. Written in his hard-to-decipher handwriting, it hadn't been the most reassuring note. She'd had one of those before. She pushed the memory away.

"What was so pressing that Doc called you to his warehouse?"

Ria could feel Drake tense, and she readied herself for the rejection to come. Only, it didn't. She snuck a peak at him as he was now intensely studying the oven door. He shot her a glance, winked, and got to work.

"We had a situation with a lone wolf." He pulled the pan out of the oven. "Tim was attacked in the middle of downtown. Doc had to stitch him up."

"And the lone wolf?"

"We have him contained."

Ria stood back as Drake placed the food onto the hot pads she'd put down on the island. He headed back to get the rest out of the oven. Something told her there was more to this story, but she didn't push. She could feel all the ears in the house pricked forward and quivering for more information.

The good part about living among the Pack: there were no secrets. The bad part about living among the Pack: there were no secrets. He raised an eyebrow as the second oven's timer dinged.

"Think you made enough?" he asked, as he lifted out a few more pans.

"Maybe." She watched him close the oven with a practiced hip bump. "I didn't know whether you'd come alone…"

How to explain the nervous, panicked energy that had filled her when she saw his note? Combined with the hangdog expressions of the sentries who were at the house, it had propelled her into the kitchen to burn it off. Werewolf business really wasn't that much different from human business except that werewolves tended to have fangs and fur involved.

Drake cocked his head to the side in a wolf-like movement as her words trailed off. "Duly noted. Next time, I'll keep you up to date." He grabbed a plate and took the serving spoon she held out as she struggled to wrap her brain around the words *next time*.

Next time. There was no guarantee that there'd be a next time. Just because he'd declared that she was his mate didn't mean she had to accept his claim. Her parents had loved each other but they'd ended up not having forever. Werewolves might be long-lived but even they couldn't survive being decapitated and cut in two. She'd woken up to a note on that night, too.

She stood rooted to the spot as Drake put together dinner for the both of them. Her fingertips tingled and felt numb, and Ria resisted the urge to shake them out. Perhaps she should just head home. Spending the day with Drake, well, she'd given into the longing—but what would happen the next time he had to disappear from the house? What would happen if he didn't come back? Panic, old and new, coalesced into the cold sweat, inducing fear she was experiencing for the first time. It all but knocked her off her feet.

Her father's grieving face was a permanent fixture in her mind. He'd tried after her mother had died in the accident, but he'd never been the same. Ria stared at Drake's back and willed herself to calm down. There was no way he hadn't noticed the fear that had flooded the room, but still, he kept his back turned.

"I'm not so sure that we will be able to get anything from the wolf. He wasn't up to an interrogation. I left him with Doc under heavy surveillance." Drake set their plates aside and Ria tensed as he turned around to face her.

"Until I find out why this is happening, I need the Pack to be careful." He leaned against the counter, his arms crossed over his chest and his eyes boring into hers.

"Why is that?"

"It's unusual for a lone wolf to attack another wolf out in the open, surrounded by humans. It's even more so for them to attack a juvenile."

Panic faded to concern. "Is Tim here or at his parents?"

"He's here." Drake smiled.

"He should be home."

"You know he's not a pup, right?"

"He's still their kid." Ria shook her head. "I would want my child to be home if he was attacked. Juvenile wolf or not."

"He's fine. A little shaken and more than a little happy to be here, where he can sample some of your home-cooked food."

"A little shaken?" Ria knew from experience it could mean anything from an already healed wound or something that required a wolf to change back and forth between states. She eyed her Alpha and wondered whether she'd have a sick wolf to tend to. Those could be dangerous, snapping with their sharp teeth at a lowly human like herself. "Did he need to change?"

"Not until he has something to eat. Then his stitches will need to come out."

"Does he need a nurse?"

"We've only ever allowed you to care for those who weren't truly a danger to you. Tim won't need a nurse and we won't have to worry about an uncontrollable wolf. If he were…"

"You would have left him at Doc's."

Drake took the few steps to reach her. He tipped up her chin and laid the barest of kisses on her lips before he wrapped his arms around her. She wasn't sure what had brought this on, but she gave in to the need and leaned into his chest and let him hold her.

The kitchen door opened. Wolf by wolf, they trickled in, drawn by the scent of food. Ria expected Drake to let her go. Instead, he held her closer. As the Pack flowed in and around them, he held her. Just held her, while the Pack took note.

***

It wasn't until they were settled in on his couch again and she'd gotten halfway through her plate that he spoke.

"Do you have vacation time?"

Poised to take a bite of chicken, Ria put it back down. "I do. Why?"

"I'd like you take time off."

This was new. Drake never asked for anything as the Alpha. It might sound to an outsider as if he had, but this was an order.

"You want me to take time off for what?" She had an inkling of what he wanted, but Ria wasn't about to let him dictate when she took time off from work.

Drake took the plate from her and placed it on his battered coffee table. When he faced her, his eyes had turned to a bright yellow. The veins on his forearms stood out and his voice, his voice when he spoke was barely human.

"I'm the Alpha. I get busy, and in order for me to be able to court you, one of us has to be available."

She blinked up at him. "You didn't just say that to me." *Submissive, Beta, not even Beta, Omega. She was lowest of the low.*

There was only one way she knew of even in the human world to establish some sort of respect, and it was to stand up for herself. The only difference was that in the Pack she just might end up ranked even lower. "You expect me to be available...whenever."

He sat back. The intensity of his gaze had her pinned to the seat. It took all she had to keep eye contact. If she had any sense, she would show him her throat in surrender. Something deep inside her refused to give in. She knew if she gave in now, she would be giving in for the rest of her life.

"Do you remember who I am?"

"I'm pretty sure some spoiled celebrity is wondering who stole their line right now." She pushed herself off the couch and made her way to the door on shaky legs, brushing past him as he gazed down at her in what she was sure was amazement. "I have work tomorrow."

She was surprised that she made it to the front door without him stopping her. Surprised and disappointed.

Paolo emerged from the game room, pool cue in

hand. "You are the only person I know that can get Drake into this mood."

Ria didn't slow down as he fell in beside her.

"What mood? Annoyed?"

"Annoyed, frustrated, confused..." He leaned against the door and kept an eye on the hallway while talking. "You can pretend all you want, but you'll end up mated to him." Paolo looked straight at her. "He needs you. This Pack needs you. Don't listen to the idiots that like to treat you like a submissive wolf, Ria. They don't know shit."

Paolo moved away as Drake's bedroom door slammed. Drake was coming after all. She stood silently by the front door, her back turned to the man who would make her his mate.

Drake reached out and opened the door for her and she stepped through, making her way to the truck. The heat of Drake's hand at the base of her spine burned its way into her memory as he guided her to the truck.

Ria's nerves felt stretched to the breaking point. She could almost feel her heart beating out of her chest. She was aware of every move he made as he backed the truck out of the driveway. He said nothing.

His eyes never left the road, his hands strong and steady on the wheel. He'd always been that way. He always knew in which direction to take the Pack. It was hard to believe that he was older than he looked. He'd already been Alpha when she was a child. Very few questioned him, except the old guard, his advisors. It was a measure of his competence that he needed so little input.

"Why me?" she asked.

He snarled in frustration at her question.

"Why not one of the other females of the Pack?"

He glanced in her direction. "Until recently, you've never run from me. You've always given me your honest opinion." He let out a gruff laugh. "What I mean to say is, I've been aware of you for most of your life. As a kid, as a teenager..."

The way he said teenager made her wonder just how aware he'd been, but he spoke before she could ask. "I knew the moment when you first became interested in me."

Her face flamed, so she turned away from him

to face the window, as she recalled the moment herself. Drake had been away. James had said Ria had the right touch when it came to making spaces cozy. In her need for acceptance, Ria had decided to prep Pack Central for the Alpha's return, cleaning up the mess his sentries had made, managing to rope them into helping. Drake's room, however, she'd handled herself.

The thing about large houses was, you never knew who was coming and going, if you were human. She'd forgotten the duvet in the dryer and had hurried back, sure she had time to fix it before the Alpha returned. She'd thrown the duvet on his bed and had been giving it one last smoothing pat, when he'd walked out of the bathroom.

Her heart was beating the same rhythm it had on that day. She closed her eyes in an effort to block out the image of him glistening with water, roughly toweling off his hair.

"Why were you the one elected to get my room ready?" Drake asked, as he slowed for a red light.

Her eyes shot open. "That was no mistake. You knew I was there, and you walked out of the shower deliberately."

"I knew you were in the room. Yes."

She waited. He said nothing more. So she braved it and asked. "Did James set me up?"

He chuckled. "James was playing matchmaker. Before you ask why, he knows that I've wanted you for mine."

"If James knows...?"

"Does everyone know? No. You've stayed away from me, and I've kept my distance, too."

"Why? Don't werewolf mates know immediately? Why wait?"

"You wanted me to jump your bones the minute I realized that you were attracted to me?" He shook his head.

Ria realized they weren't on the way to her place. In fact, they'd been driving aimlessly, but it looked like he was now headed back to his house.

"What do you think you're doing? I made it clear I wanted to go back to my house."

"You're mine. I've waited five years to make my move. Longer than that, if you need to know."

"What?"

"I've wanted you since you were seventeen. You walked out of that pool in that bikini, and I was lost."

"I've only had one bikini. My mother threw it out after..."

"Yeah, that one. Your father threatened to kill me if I laid a hand on you."

"You were his Alpha."

"That doesn't give me the right to lust after his seventeen-year-old daughter."

Her head fell back against the seat. "Is that why my parents shipped me off to prep school and then college?"

He growled. "Yes. They wanted to make sure you saw some of the world before I got my hands on you."

"What would have happened if I'd gotten married?"

The steering wheel creaked as leather and wood began to split under the force of Drake's grip.

She loved him, or at the least infatuation had grown into something stronger. She'd spent so much time thinking of herself as human that she wasn't sure if she would know how to recognize the signs of a mating for her wolf half. If she went with the premise that she was only human, was feeling the way she did right now enough to commit herself to Drake?

She had no one to ask. Her human friends were actually close acquaintances or coworkers who knew not to ask too many questions. They would think it was odd, anyway, if she asked them about love. And the Pack, the Pack was nothing more than a bunch of gossips. If she asked one, then all of them would know.

She let out a frustrated growl.

"You agreed to give me a chance. I'm asking for it again, Ria. I need for you to trust me."

"And what happens if this doesn't work?"

"Then I let you walk away."

Ria finally looked over at him. His eyes were wolf bright, his body tense with trying to hold back. She could see the effort it cost him not to just impose his will. She'd forgotten a wolf's drive to pursue its prey, and in the forgetting, she'd pushed him to fight his instinct. While he was circling back to the house, she knew if she asked, he would turn around and drive her to her house. But she couldn't keep torturing either of them.

"I don't know if I'll ever have the same mating instinct you have."

"You're half wolf, Ria, but you're also human, and both sides believe in love."

"Love?"

"Love and mating are basically the same thing, aren't they?"

"Except that mating is for life and..."

"And if done right, love is, too."

He was right. Mating might be something a wolf couldn't escape. But love was both a feeling and a choice. If done right, both would last for a lifetime. She and Drake both deserved to know where this was headed. And she had to be the one brave enough to say yes.

Ria licked her lips, swallowed and took the leap. "I'm willing to find out."

The ride back was silent. The only sound that filled the cab was that of their breathing. She could only stare straight ahead at the road she knew would take them to his home. The sound of her heartbeat filled her ears as they drove up to the house. Drake opened the SUV's door for her.

He stood, his hand out, waiting for her to take his.

"Thank you." Her voice sounded rusty to her ears as her palm slid into place against his much-larger, callused one.

"You're welcome." His response rumbled through her body, adding tremors as it went. Low and gravelly, it drew her even closer to him. They stood there, between the door and the SUV, their bodies touching, breath mingling, her hand still in his. They were in full view of the Pack. Ria ducked her head, and the moment broke.

As he led her through the house, they were both silent. Neither made a sound until they were in his suite. Drake's face was a hard mask. His eyes searched her face even as his nostrils flared. Ria wondered what he scented. Was it her desire, or her fear?

She licked her lips as she watched him deliberately turn, close the door and engage the lock. He stood tall and strong before her. Ria's palms itched to touch him. She twisted her purse strap instead. He moved closer, his eyes trained on hers. Ria released her grip on her purse and heard it hit the floor as his hands glided along her cheeks to cup her face.

Drake covered her lips with his. Ria gave in and let the world fall away, held in place by his lips on hers. She sucked in air when Drake lifted his lips from hers. Her eyes were slower to comply, but her lids lifted and she found herself gazing in to his glowing eyes. They were bright in a face hardened by passion. Ria breathed in a shaky breath as she held his gaze. When he looked at her with that much heat and longing, Ria knew he was holding back. Judging by the gentle way he touched her, he was afraid he would hurt her.

Ria closed her eyes as Drake's fingers slid down her arms to capture hers. He drew her into his bedroom, stopping only to close the doors, giving them another layer of privacy before he took her mouth again. Ria lost herself in Drake's taste, the feel of his tongue against hers driving her higher. Her hands crept up the front of his shirt. Her fingers slipped upward, caressing skin and slipping into his silky hair as he pulled her closer. Drake's body was hard against hers, and she melted into him. She didn't fight it anymore and let every bit of her wanting for him pour free.

The backs of her legs hit the bed as Drake let her free with a growl. His eyes, wolfbright, kept her attention until he began to trace her skin with his fingertips, his hands shaking. He was tracing where her shoulder met her neck, one of the places she would love to feel his teeth. She shivered under his scrutiny and tilted her head to give him greater access. Ria couldn't stop the cry that erupted from her lips as Drake's lips followed his fingers.

His hands stopped moving. Ria opened her eyes. Instead of feeling like a cornered fox at the end of a hunt, she felt exhilarated and safe at the same time. A fuzzy knowledge filled her head. He thought she was beautiful. *Closer.*

Closer. It sounded like Drake, but neither of them had spoken. He began tugging his shirt up. She wanted skin. His skin, against hers. When he reached down and picked her up, Ria gladly wrapped her legs around his hips and let him lay her down on the bed. And as soon as her back touched the bed, her hands were busy again.

Her fingertips met the hot, hard plane of his abs. Drake sucked in a breath above her and sat back from her. He was beautiful to behold:skin slightly tanned from all the time he spent in the sun, not an ounce of fat on him, one or two scars from injuries that hadn't healed right the first time.

Ria's hands dipped lower. His eyes closed as she traced a line down his stomach. Here she held power. It made her bold to see him still and powerful atop her. She kept going, undoing his belt and jeans. Slipping her hand inside. Smiling in triumph as her hand closed over her prize. Only to have his hand close over hers and squeeze, moving her hand up and down his shaft. Ria reveled in the expression on his face.

Drake's eyes opened, and Ria felt her heart rate pick up. Gently, he removed her hand and backed off the bed to shed his jeans in record time. *Commando*. She couldn't help the grin that spread across her face.

He crooked an eyebrow at her. "I'm not going to be the only one naked here." He gripped her ankle and pulled her down to the edge of the bed with a grin of his own. It turned wicked. Once he divested her of her boots and pants, he made quick work of her top and bra. He wanted nothing in his way. Drake smoothed his hands up her calves, up her thighs, and traced the line of her thong. "So this is what's under your work clothes? I like."

His head was bent, poised to deliver a kiss to her stomach. Ria laid back. Her body bare, except for a cotton thong and a wolf at her stomach.

Drake nuzzled her stomach and dropped a kiss there before crawling up her body. Inch by slow delicious inch, with his eyes locked on hers, he pushed himself between her legs. Ria arched up to meet him, greedy for his touch.

If he was right about her being his mate, this was the way it was supposed to be. If he wasn't, then she was grabbing at this with both hands and taking it all while she could. She loved him. She always would.

The only sounds in the darkened room were their breathing and skin connecting with skin. Ria held fast to the man who drew her closer and closer to ecstasy with every touch and kiss. She reveled in the way he touched her. His hands were firm but careful.

Mine.

The word reverberated through her body just as Drake pushed her over the edge. She felt it deep inside her. Ria came back to earth slowly, aware that Drake was watching her. He was still hard inside her. Waiting for her to come back so he could do it again, and she was willing to do it all again.

Except she was sure of one thing, he hadn't spoken the word *mine.* In fact, her eyes had been wide open and she'd been looking at him.

His eyes focused, jaw locked tight as he watched her go over again. She could feel him waiting as he nuzzled the underside of her jaw. He made a contented sound and settled into a slow rhythm.

Ria's hips rolled under his, drawn into a dance with a very certain outcome. He licked at her neck again. The wolf was listening intently to her heart beat, and the man was ready to sink his teeth into the place where her neck and shoulder met. Eager to mark her as his.

She tilted her neck and felt the wave of satisfaction, possession and triumph that rushed through him. When his fangs closed over her skin, she rode the wave of rightness into oblivion.

CHAPTER FIVE

Ria woke to Drake leaving the bed. She studied his body as he moved to the door of the suite. Muscles bunched and rippled. She sat up, ready to suggest a pair of pants, when it struck her that she'd have to get used to his nudity. Werewolves weren't exactly known for their modesty. Still, she was relieved when he grabbed a pair of pajama bottoms from the bottom of the night stand.

He opened the door, but not before shooting her a smile. He'd probably heard her eyelids open. She chuckled, wrapping the sheets around herself more securely.

Then Ria realized that James stood in the doorway, sheepishly avoiding her gaze. There was no way for her to get out and get dressed without James seeing her naked behind. She was trapped. Ria ducked under the comforter Drake had thrown over her. She made herself as small as possible, until she was sure nothing, not even the top of her head, could be seen from the door.

The sound of Drake closing the pocket doors to the bedroom followed. Ria popped her head above the covers and immediately began to grab her clothing, while keeping an ear on the conversation through the door.

"What's going on?" Drake asked his second.

"Doc called. The wolf is stabilized. We might be able to get some answers. You said you wanted to be there."

Fully dressed and doing her best to control her now-tousled curls, Ria eased the door open and caught James' eye. Curiosity and concern trumped her embarrassment. She stood just behind Drake and listened to them discuss Pack business.

"Is Tim okay?"

"He's fine, the meal Ria had ready plus some raw meat did him good. His parents already picked him up."

She hesitated a beat before asking, "Do we know why he was attacked?"

"No, hopefully we'll find that out now."

Drake reached back and drew her to his side,

sliding an arm around her waist. Ria stilled at his touch. Drake dipped his head and inhaled her scent mixed with his, combined with fear and hope. He dropped a kiss on her shoulder.

James moved out into the hallway, giving them a small bit of privacy.

Drake nuzzled her neck as the pressure of his hands on her hips increased. He turned her to face him. Ria glanced at the door. "Easy."

He cupped her face between his hands. "My wolf feels the need to mark you, even if it's just James who's been talking to you."

Ria closed her eyes as he traced the mark he made on her neck. She could swear she felt his regret and his reluctance at leaving her, even as her body softened and leaned into his.

"I'll be back."

"Be safe." She didn't let the words go that she'd held inside for years. She was afraid to. Instead, she leaned forward and caught his lips in a gentle kiss that was filled with everything she wanted to say.

James coughed from the doorway.

Drake smiled against her mouth and pulled

back. "I will."

***

"They pumped him full of something," Doc said.

He and Drake stood side by side, Doc with his shirtsleeves rolled up and arms folded as he contemplated the cage in front of them. The silver bars weakened anyone attempting to get out.

"Do you know with what?" Drake smelled the frustration coming off of Doc. The expert was stumped, and that didn't make Drake feel any better. He had a lone wolf with a hair trigger in his territory, hopped up on some sort of designer drug. "Do you think it's out of his system?"

"I don't know. We can't let him out. It took a hell of a lot to just get blood from him."

Doc held up his rapidly healing arm. To anyone else, the slight red marks wouldn't mean anything, but to a wolf, it meant that Doc had almost lost a good chunk of his arm in the attempt.

"What you're saying is, he's out of his mind. And, we have no way of knowing what his state of mind was before he or whoever the hell it was pumped him full of an unknown drug."

"Yes, and he's a dominant lone wolf who isn't inclined toward the friendly." Doc rubbed at the redness of his arm is if reliving the attack.

"Shit."

"If we can't get him to cooperate, you may have to break him to keep him in line."

Drake frowned. Turning a dominant into a quivering, weakened mass wasn't something he wanted to do. Other Alphas would relish bringing another dominant to his knees. Some would even go as far as killing a wolf without a reason. "Find another way."

"I'm trying, but you're probably going to have to."

"Doc, do what you can. I'd hate to break a dominant unnecessarily."

Visions of another wolf squirming under his compulsion on a concrete floor filled Drake's mind. That wolf had fought with everything he had. Sweat had trickled down Drake's spine. In the end, Drake had won, but at the cost of a wolf who'd never been the same again. A shadow under his current Alpha, he was kept under constant suicide watch.

Doc donned protective gloves, then checked the sleeping wolf's vitals through the bars of the cage. "I know you don't want to. It's why the Pack accepted you as their Alpha. You don't go the easy route. Dominance for the sake of dominance was never your thing."

Drake headed down the hall to Doc's office. This wasn't how he'd intended to spend the night. Swearing, he dialed the number to the lab the Pack owned. "I need a full work up. Yes, I know you did one, but I need another. It may be something new. Check the databases."

Drake got up from the chair when Doc called down the hall. "He's shifted."

A fairly large male was hunkered down on the floor of the cage, clutching Doc's gloved arm in his mouth. Drake slowed his steps and stayed out of sight. The male had shredded Doc's specially designed gloves, so if Doc touched the bars while withdrawing his arm, he'd be in pain. The damage from the silver would be considerable.

Drake walked out into the open. "Let his arm go."

Startled, the man did just that. Doc withdrew his hand from the cage. Quickly, he stripped off the glove and checked the bandage beneath. Drake waited to see if any extra damage had been caused. When Doc shook his head, Drake switched his attention to the cage. The lone man was dazed, sitting in a half-crouch.

"Who are you?"

It took the loner a while to answer. It was as if he had to slog through whatever drug was pumping through his system. He shook his head as if to clear it. "My name is Patrick."

"Patrick, where are you from?"

He shook his head again, but didn't answer.

Drake checked Patrick's eyes. They hadn't gone wolf. He hoped that was a good sign. He tried again. "Why are you in my territory?"

He didn't get an answer. Silently, Drake cursed. Doc shook his head from the other side of the cage while he wielded a chip reader. Patrick wasn't chipped. Most packs were, though there were a few who held out against it. Shifting presented a unique problem, causing wolves to lose their ID along with their clothes. In order to identify a shifter, they had to rely on the same technology vets used for dogs and cats. Hell, they had a network of "vets" that specialized in unusual animals, which was what the chips read if a human vet discovered them.

Patrick smelled of desert, yet his accent denoted the south, which was confusing. Georgia's Alpha kept a tight rein on things. There was no way this lone wolf had come out of there. That left the Carolinas, an easy place to hide out. That could explain the accent, but it still didn't explain the scent of desert.

Patrick's legs gave out and he collapsed against the floor of the cage. There was no way Drake could question him now.

Doc moved to unlock the cage. "I'll let him out and get him into the room."

Drake reached out to stop him. "He just tore your arm open. You let him out and he attacks you again, I will break him or kill him. I won't have a choice."

Doc looked at his quickly healing arm, the skin knitting back together. "He's a patient. He's a man in need of my help. I can do my best with him in the cage, but the silver is not helping his recovery. In fact, it may be preventing it."

Drake took another look at the male on the bottom of the cage. He wasn't opposed to treating his captive as a human being. However, he also had to think of the Pack. "You may be a werewolf, but you can still be put out of commission. I'll do what I have to do to keep you safe. Let's get him out of there."

Together, they moved him to one of the few rooms Doc had outfitted for less dangerous wolves, with Drake cursing all the way because he'd gotten too close to the bars. The son of a bitch was heavy. Drake was ashamed to admit it, but they dumped him onto the hospital bed instead of moving him gently. Sweating, with his side stinging, he watched as Doc drew more blood and checked his patient's vitals. Doc looked up through his hair. "I told you we need a gurney in here."

Drake swiped at his forehead. "I'll increase your budget."

"Good, because I already ordered it."

"Taking advantage of your position again, Doc?"

"Hey, I've known you since you were in diapers, boy. Why don't you get back to your mate and leave this old man in peace?"

***

Ria tried going back to bed, but it felt empty without Drake. She didn't like not knowing what was going on. They'd have to have a talk when he got back about that—and about the mating bond. Ria could almost feel it kicking in. It was like a whisper, something that she could just barely glimpse out of the corner of her eye.

Her mother had spoken of it once. It'd been one of the few times Ria had come home during college. They'd had a movie marathon, just the two of them, while her father had run with the Pack.

"It's like love and knowledge all rolled up in one. You know when he's safe and when he's not. It ties you closer than you can imagine."

"Can he sense you, too?"

Her mother had smiled, popped another kernel in her mouth, and nodded before picking up the remote control. "One day, you'll feel it, and you'll realize it's indescribably beautiful."

Little had Ria known that her mother had been talking about Drake. That they'd purposefully kept Ria away from him. Oh, she understood now that their silence had been their way to give her a chance to see the world. To experience life.

It had been for the best, yet it had left her feeling horribly alone when her parents had died in the car crash. Sometimes she got angry that they'd left her alone.

She threw off the covers and headed for the shower, picking up her clothes as she went. The bathroom in here had always called to her. It showed the personality of its owner. Hedonistic, with a large walk-in shower dominating one side with a rainfall shower head and numerous massage jets. There was a huge Jacuzzi bath under what she knew were heavily tinted windows, but she drew the blinds, anyway.

She looked longingly at the bath, but turned on the shower. Her stomach had begun growling a few minutes ago. Sighing, she stepped under the water. Her heart hurt, and she should have told Drake she loved him. She still hid, though what she wanted was in easy reach.

He was out dealing with a potentially dangerous situation. She was worried, never mind that he'd told her not to worry. She knew he was dominant, powerfully so. Her father had always said it was better for all involved if they recognized him as Alpha. Drake had the ability to break anyone in the Pack, although, to her knowledge, he very rarely used it. It hurt him to use it, so he found other ways to steer the Pack in the direction he wanted.

Closing her eyes, she poured shampoo into her hand and began to lather her hair.

***

Drake growled in frustration as he checked his phone. Ria wasn't answering. He reminded himself that she was safe at the house. Someone would brave the Alpha's bedroom to let her know what was going on.

Drake and the sentries secured the warehouse. No one was to be allowed in or out. While they waited on James to call, he and Doc discussed the future of the sleeping lone wolf. An Alpha decided a lone wolf's ability to stay in his territory.

"We don't know the effect this drug will have on him in the long term." Doc scratched the back of his neck while he looked over the lab reports.

"If he's strong enough, I wouldn't want to hold him here." Drake folded his arms over his chest and leaned against the wall. "I don't want a wolf in my Pack that doesn't want to be here. I can't hold a pack of this size together if I'm holding them by force."

Drake's vibrated in his pocket. He pulled it out and answered.

"James."

Doc turned back to the bed but no doubt he had his ears pricked for information. James had taken off to investigate the alert concerning one of their safe houses. There were several in the city, all within thirty minutes of each other and close to the highway.

Designated by numbers, this one was simply

know as number three. Except for a few sentries, it didn't see much action, unlike Doc's. While it could have been a break in, it was more than likely a test. Though the lone wolves had only been sporadic, something in Drake's gut told him this was linked to the man who lay unconscious in the bed.

"Alpha." He could hear James' footfalls as he walked across the parking lot. Drake's wolf prowled within. Something was wrong. "It was a false alarm. Sheena sent the alert. Drake, she's alone at the house with Ria."

"I want my mate safe. Get to the house." Rubber pealing out on asphalt was the sound which met his command.

Drake took off for his own SUV at a run.

***

Ria groaned as hot water slid over her body. She was deliciously sore in some places, and memories of just how she got that way brought a blush to her face. The click of claws on tile caused her to look up. An unfamiliar shadow paused in front of the glass blocks. Ria fought to keep her breathing slow and even. Ria hoped like hell the sound of the water hitting the tiled floor hid her increased heart rate.

The wolf wasn't Drake. It was either playing with her or was too excited to care that it made noise. Ria kept her eyes on the enemy. She had one chance at survival. Humming as if she didn't have a care in the world she slid to the right as the shadow moved left. Out from under the shower, she used her momentum to move as far as she could and ended up just under the towel bar.

Ria grabbed hold of the only weapon she could and pulled, all the while praying that adrenaline and the wolf half of her genetics would give her just enough of an edge to pull the bar free. It came loose. Her hands stung even as she tightened her slick grip on the towel rod. Ria kept her back to the wall and an eye on the dirty blonde wolf that sat on the opposite side of the shower.

Drake's wolf was bigger, black as midnight. The blonde wolf rose from its haunches and closed the distance between them. Cocky, but damn sure not a male. She was smaller than any male werewolf Ria had seen. Ria gripped the towel rack and waited for her chance.

She'd only get one.

The wolf came closer. It passed through the stream of water Ria had left running. It paused at the edge of the shower with its eyes narrowed, head lowered. Ria waited and watched as muscles bunched under wet fur. She held her ground until the last moment. Ria got a set of stripes from the wolf's claws for her effort, but she brought the towel rod down, hard. She hit her target, but all it earned her was a yelp but not much else.

Ria backed away. Taking her eye off of her opponent wasn't an option. Ria hadn't managed to stun the wolf, but she'd drawn blood. At least she'd gotten a little of her own back. Panic crawled up her spine. One thought scared her more than any other. She was in a house full of werewolves, yet no one was coming to rescue her.

"Who are you?"

The she-wolf smiled. She, definitely she, there was no male genitalia in evidence. Ria wracked her brain to figure out which female would want her dead?

"You know this isn't exactly a smart move."

The she-wolf moved forward. Too late, Ria realized what it was doing. It was herding her into the closet. *Shit! Classic, stupid move.*

"You know, attacking me means that Drake will come after you. He'll have help. James will be right at his side." Ria reached back. She moved her left hand blindly, in a futile attempt to look for something other than the bar she currently held. Nothing. Shoes. Shirts. She was on her own.

The wolf stopped advancing. Its ears swiveled. A horrible creaking filled the bathroom seconds before the solid wooden door splintered apart under the paws of a snarling wolf.

Ria flinched and dove to the floor. She threw her arms over her head and turned her body away in an attempt to shield herself from the shrapnel. That instinctive move had made her take her eyes off of the enemy.

Ria paid for it in blood. Claws ripped into her shoulders. Digging deep, they unleashed screams from her throat. Ria rolled and her back hit the tile as a mass of wet fur, claws and teeth followed her down. Ria pushed up and away, keeping the she-wolf from taking a bite out of her.

***

Drake couldn't stop the enraged howl that rose up his throat as Sheena bucked from Ria kicking under her. He sank his teeth into Sheena's scruff with deadly accuracy, yanking her off Ria. He threw her aside. Sheena hit the wall with a thud. He began his shift the moment Sheena's unconscious body hit the floor. Ria sat up and moved away from Drake as he shifted. His amber eyes glowed and held her own while his muscles shifted under fur that receded. His claws turned into fingers on the tile.

"Ria!"

Her eyes were barely open. Gently, he inspected her injuries, flinching when she whimpered at his touch. His heart threatened to beat right through his chest. She looked so small, crumpled against the wall. His wolf wanted to go back and tear Sheena apart limb by limb for touching his mate. Ria whimpered again and the wolf and the man were in agreement: Ria came first. Vengeance would come later.

Drake reached down. "Sweetheart, I'm going to move you."

He heard booted feet hit the tile. His backup had arrived.

"I'll get Doc," Tim said, turning and rushing out the way he'd come.

"Here." Paolo grabbed a stack of towels. "Press this against the wound. Shit, she's going to need stitches."

"Doc's on his way." Drake took the towels he offered and tried to staunch the bleeding.

James stepped in and took charge of the cleanup, a good thing, since all Drake could see was his injured mate bleeding on the floor. "Paolo, I need you to take care of Sheena. She's unconscious, and we don't know what injuries she's sustained. We need her contained. Tim's waiting at the front door for Doc."

Drake gathered Ria up into his arms and took her into the bedroom. Someone had covered the bed in towels. He laid a dazed Ria on the bed just as Tim escorted Doc into the room.

***

They wouldn't allow him into the room. Drake paced the hallway in a pair of sweatpants someone handed him, his feet bare against the cool tile. Ria's blood stained his hands and chest. Both he and his wolf were in agreement once more: their heart was in the next room. They'd let the enemy attack her.

James leaned against the doorjamb, watching him pace. "She'll be fine."

Drake hoped James was right. He could feel her through the mate bond. She was passed out. Weak, tired, and when she woke, she'd be pissed. Pride and rage mixed inside of him. The entire drive to the house, he'd been helpless. The only thing that had kept him sane was the mate bond. Through it, he'd felt her heart beating and known she was alive.

Still, the Pack had been betrayed by one of its own. Drake's skin rippled as he reined in his instinct to change. He focused on something else, something that had been bothering him since he'd broken into the bathroom. Something his nose had told him. "Patrick."

"What about Patrick?" James took a step away from the door jamb.

Drake closed his eyes as he listened to instinct. Sheena smelled like Patrick. "Once Doc is finished here, I need him to check Sheena's blood work. I want to see if the drugs found in Patrick's system match what I think is in Sheena's system." Drake felt his nails elongate into claws. "I want to know what drove Sheena to attack her Alpha's mate."

Drake didn't wait for James to reply. He turned and yanked open the door.

Doc turned toward the door and met Drake's eyes. "I wondered how long James could hold you out there."

Drake didn't bother with a response. Ria's pale form drew him like a lodestone.

"She'll have a few scars, since she's half human," Doc stated, as he tied off the suture he was working on. "But other than that, she'll be fine."

"What about all the blood she lost?"

"Funny thing, her being half werewolf. She

heals much more quickly than a regular human. Didn't even require a transfusion." Doc picked up his bag and headed toward the door. "I'll be back to check on her in a while."

Drake sat on the bed, holding Ria's hand. Drake prayed hard while he waited for Ria to open her eyes. There was no one he trusted more than Doc to take care of his mate, but to have finally joined with his mate and then almost lose her in such a short period of time was harder than he could have known. He felt like he needed extra help. Drake rested his head against the mattress and prayed harder.

He dreamt of her running her fingers through his hair. He opened his eyes to find hers locked on him. His heart stuttered.

"Hi." She smiled, and he breathed again.

"How are you feeling?" His voice sounded strained even to his ears. Footsteps sounded in the hall. "Hold that thought. I think Doc's here to see you."

Doc knocked on the door a moment later, entering the room without waiting for permission.

"Awake? Good, good. Drake, get off that bed. It

can't be comfortable for her." Doc made quick work of checking her out. Drake felt the pressure in his chest ease as Doc pulled the cover back up over Ria. "You know it would be better if you could change, young lady. Then those..." He gestured to the stiches that held the wounds on her shoulders closed. "...wouldn't be necessary. Ah, well, they're healing well, though."

"So she's fine?"

Doc looked only slightly annoyed at the question. "Yes. But I have something else to talk to you about." Doc moved out into the hallway.

Drake rubbed his thumb against the back of her hand. "I'll be back. Need to talk to Doc." At the puzzled look in her brown eyes, he smiled. "I'll tell you later."

Drake followed Doc out into the hallway. "Let's hear it."

"You were right, that mystery chemical was in Sheena's blood as well."

"And none of the other labs had a signature on it?"

"No."

"One or more of them could be lying, especially if another pack wants to take over our territory." Drake leaned against the wall of the hallway and crossed his arms over his chest while he mulled the situation over. "James?"

James rounded the corner immediately.

Knowing his second had heard every word, Drake wasted no time in addressing him. "I haven't heard of any of the other Alphas wanting this territory. Most have a hard enough time with trying to run their own cities. Why tackle Orlando? I want intel. This is just the beginning."

"We have another problem," James reported. "We can't find Trina."

"No one's seen her?"

"That's just it, Drake, the only person she hung around with was Sheena."

Drake pushed off the wall. "We can't contact her Alpha before we know the facts. Has anyone searched Sheena's apartment?"

"Paolo's over there now."

"Good. I don't want to wait too long to send out a search team. Her pack will want to look for her, too. She could be another victim of Sheena's, or Trina could have slipped Sheena the drug. I want to know if she is innocent or working under orders from her Alpha or someone else."

At James questioning look, he grimaced. "I know, James. But I've got to cover every possible angle. Besides, isn't this exactly why you chose not to contest my claim?"

"Damn straight. I don't have your touch for diplomacy."

Doc barked out a laugh. "If you think Drake's diplomatic, my boy, it's a good thing you're his second. I'd hate to see what you'd consider diplomacy." He hitched his satchel over his shoulder and turned to leave. He clapped his hand on Drake's shoulder. "You'll deal with this the way it ought to be. Don't second guess yourself."

Drake nodded, knowing he wasn't fooling Doc. He wanted blood, and Doc knew it.

***

Three days later, Ria emerged from the guest

room. Stiff, sore, and thoroughly tired of that bed, she wrapped her robe around her. She'd barely made it two steps out the door when one of the Pack ratted her out.

"Drake! She's up!" Carly, a barely out of her teens she-wolf, stuck her tongue out at one of the younger females, who in turn surprised Ria with a quick brush of cheek against cheek.

Ria stood frozen to the spot with shock. She'd never had another Pack member greet her like that. It implied trust and belonging. Ria touched her cheek. Her eyes filled with tears.

"Did I hurt you?" The affectionate female gave Ria a quick once over. "Did I bump your stiches? I'm so sorry. Here he comes. He's going to kill me for hurting you."

"Did you hurt my mate?" Drake asked the young girl. "I don't smell pain."

The juvenile female beat a hasty retreat, leaving them standing in hall alone. That was, if Ria didn't count the various werewolves with super-sensitive hearing roaming the house and grounds. Ria silently thanked the gods Drake had had the foresight to soundproof the Alpha's suite.

He herded her back to their suite without touching her. Ria's skinned ached to feel his touch. Her heart ached because she knew he was afraid to touch her. She'd needed him to hold her every time she'd woken in the past couple of days.

"When are you going to touch me?" The words spilled from her lips, and it was as if the floodgates had opened. "I need you, Drake. I'm not a delicate piece of glass."

Somewhere deep inside of her, she felt his overwhelming relief that she was okay. For a second, she also knew his panic that she might not be healing as she should be and his fear of hurting her, but then the mate bond closed again. The bond would get stronger the longer they were mated. As new as it was, it fluctuated.

"Ria."

The slide of Drake's palms against her cheeks was enough to make her shut her eyes. She didn't know what he'd felt when the bond had opened up, but if it led to him touching her again, then she was all for it. Drake's lips brushed over her forehead before coming to rest on hers.

"Tell me you felt it, too." His thumbs stroked over her skin. "I was trying not to hurt you, and I ended up causing you pain, anyway."

Ria opened her eyes and lifted her face to his kiss. His lips brushed against hers in the lightest, sweetest caress. Ria sighed into his kiss. She'd missed this, missed him, and when he broke their kiss off, she leaned into him, absorbing his heat and strength. Drake rested his chin on her head and curved his hands around her hips.

"I've always known you were mine." His voice rumbled in her ear. She stayed put as his fingers traced a pattern on her spine. They were still in that position when James found them.

A rueful smile eased the white lines of exhaustion in his face. "Glad to see it's final. Sorry to bother you, but we've found Trina."

Drake's smile vanished.

Ria slipped her hand in Drake's. "Go ahead, James."

"She didn't achieve her objective."

Ria felt the words clear to her soul "What would my death have achieved?"

"You still don't get it, do you?" James looked exasperated. "Besides the fact that you're the Alpha's mate. Hell, Drake, you tell her."

Drake turned her so she could see his eyes. "You're a vital part of this Pack. The only reason they haven't plagued you with their attention this week is because I've forbidden them to disturb you. You keep us together." When she opened her mouth to protest, he put a finger on her lips. "I hold them by strength of leadership and loyalty, but you hold them with heart. Yours."

She looked to James for confirmation. "Yeah, kid. They took advantage of you, but they do love you and appreciate you. Besides, most of us knew who you belonged to, even if you didn't."

"Why would Trina want the Pack to lose me, though?"

"She was supposed to destabilize the Pack, so that her Alpha could move in."

Drake asked the hardest question. "What happened when she failed?"

James was grim. "She was already dying when we found her. They staked her out with silver."

***

The master suite was being remodeled. Drake didn't want Ria reliving Sheena's attack every time she stepped into the bathroom. A giggle caught his attention. The females of the Pack had requested permission to visit Ria. Drake stood in the doorway, watching her playing peekaboo with an inquisitive toddler while talking to the pup's mother. His chest tightened as Ria looked up and met his gaze. He'd wanted his mate for so long, and for so long she had been denied him.

He scented James long before he heard him. "We need to talk."

"You've got info."

"New designer drug, formulated specifically to affect werewolves, causing them to go feral with little or no control except to obey whatever orders they've been given." James held out a sheet of paper. It turned out to be list of random animal attacks.

"Doc's been investigating those that bear a passing resemblance to wolf attacks. A quarter of them so far might be wolves on the drug."

Drake's gut rocked. It was confirmation of his worst fear. "We need to track them all down. Some of them could still be in the area. Put the word out in the Pack that all contact with lone wolves needs to be reported."

Ria's scent wafted toward him, and moments later, a small hand slid around his waist. He lifted his arm to allow her to cuddle closer, but his mate was rapidly growing into her role.

"What's going on?" she asked, but her tone was one of command, not request.

"Tell her, James." Drake waited until she'd heard it all, before he told her the rest. "We're calling an emergency circle."

"I thought only the Council could call an emergency."

"The attempted murder of an Alpha's mate is an emergency." Drake's felt the shiver go down her spine. "The death of an Alpha's mate could lead to the destabilization of a territory."

Besides him Ria whispered, "and the Council has worked too hard to keep the werewolves a secret from the human population."

***

Ria watched Drake pack for his trip to Arizona for the sentencing of the Alpha who'd ordered the attacks. Sentencing didn't really explain what being called in front of the Council for sentencing meant. It was a trial, a sentencing and the meting out of punishment all rolled into one. At least that was the way Drake had explained it to her.

Werewolf justice was nothing if not swift. But, it was also just. No punishment was decided without an investigation. The Council was nothing if not thorough.

"Will the investigator from the Council guard be there?" Ria asked, as she settled on the edge of the bed to watch Drake pack.

The Council had wanted to be sure of the Arizona Alpha's guilt and had sent out a team of investigators from what was simply known as the Guard.

The man who'd taken her statement had set the hairs on the back of her neck standing and Drake barging into the room. His partner had been no less intimidating. There was something lethal about them both.

Drake looked up from where he'd dropped his duffel. "More than likely." He strode over to where she sat and knelt between her legs. His hands slid up her jean-clad thighs. "He made you nervous."

"Yes, there is something about him. About both of them, really." She reached out and traced the line of his brow. "I know that we're werewolves and sometimes violence is necessary. I know you'd do everything in your power to protect the Pack..."

He took her hand into his and kissed her palm. "The men you met are loyal to the Council, or perhaps I should say they currently serve the Council in an investigative and peace-keeping capacity. They are highly trained wolves. Lethal. And that's what we need right now."

She stood when Drake stood. "What happens if they insist on the old ways?"

His eyes went wolf. "There is no old way, Ria."

"Death by Alpha." The words left Ria in a rush. "But none of this makes sense. Why did he want me dead?"

"I don't think the Arizona Alpha wanted you dead. At least, not initially. Between the lone wolf attacks and your attack, there's a bigger problem. We'll take it to the Council."

Ria's stomach twisted at those words. "We could be trusting the wrong people."

"Yes."

Ria took a long, hard look at her mate. "You know what you're doing. I assume you have a plan?"

"We'll draw them in and let them think we're only worried about the drug."

She heard him say "we" and felt a twinge of guilt. He was going alone, but an Alpha's mate should be by his side, even if she was half-human. Ria hated her own cowardice.

Ria walked to the closet where all of her clothes now hung and pulled out her suitcase. Drake smiled in approval when she placed it on the bed next to his duffel.

"I guess I better pack, or we'll miss the flight."

Adrenaline flooded her body. Ria was about to take her place as her Pack's Alpha female and its Alpha's mate.

THE END

ACKNOWLEDGEMNTS

None of this would have been possible without the love and support of my very large family, most specifically my husband. My Saturday writing crew, though the faces have changed due to time constraints and distance; K.C. Burn, Jeanan Glazier Davis, Jax Cassidy and Lori Sjoberg. My friends Katie Reus, Qwillia Rain and Latessa Montegomery. To Jaycee DeLorenzo and Caro Carson, I couldn't have done this without your expertise and your guidance.

ABOUT THE AUTHOR

I was born in Brooklyn New York, raised on the island of Saint Vincent and the Grenadines. According to my father, I learned to read at three and wouldn't allow him to skip a page of a story. I grew up raiding my mother's stash of books and my Aunt Patsy's extensive library. There, I developed my love of literature, and specifically romance.

Books transported me to different worlds, and encouraged me to learn about different cultures, continents, expanding my horizons. I currently live in Central Florida with my family and our interesting pet pooch Maya.

For more information, please visit my website: www.chudneythomas.com. You can also find me on twitter @CDeFthom or Facebook at https://www.facebook.com/ChudneyThomas. I can also be found on Pinterest at http://www.pinterest.com/cdefthom.

If you like to be notified of future releases please join my newsletter: http://eepurlcom/uj-yr

Made in the USA
Middletown, DE
20 April 2015